Yellow Umbrella Books are published by Capstone Press
151 Good Counsel Drive, P.O. Box 669, Mankato, Minnesota 56002
www.capstonepress.com

Library of Congress Cataloging-in-Publication Data
Catala, Ellen.
    What does a firefighter do? / by Ellen Catala.
    p. cm.
    Summary: A simple introduction to the duties of fire fighters.
    ISBN 0-7368-2911-3 (hardcover)—ISBN 0-7368-2870-2 (softcover)
    1. Fire extinction—Juvenile literature. 2. Fire fighters—Juvenile literature.
[1. Fire fighters. 2. Fire extinction. 3. Occupations.] I. Title.
TH9148.C36 2004
628.9′2—dc21   2003008675

Editorial Credits
Editorial Director: Mary Lindeen
Editor: Jennifer VanVoorst
Photo Researchers: Kelly Garvin, Wanda Winch
Developer: Raindrop Publishing

Photo Credits
Cover: Gary Sundermeyer/Capstone Press; Title Page: Myrleen Cate/Index Stock;
Page 2: Gary Sundermeyer/Capstone Press; Page 3: Corel; Page 4: Corel; Page 5:
Robert Maass/Corbis; Page 6: Steve Spak/911 Pictures; Page 7: Royalty-Free/Corbis;
Page 8: Paul M. Ross Jr./911 Pictures; Page 9: Karen Wattenmaker/911 Pictures; Page
10: Michael Heller/911 Pictures; Page 11: Bruce Ando/Index Stock; Page 12: Royalty-
Free/Corbis; Page 13: Michael Heller/911 Pictures; Page 14: Gary Sundermeyer/
Capstone Press; Page 15: Michael Heller/911 Pictures; Page 16: Comstock

1 2 3 4 5 6 09 08 07 06 05 04

What Does a Firefighter Do?

by Ellen Catala

Consultant: Mark Edelbrock, Firefighter, Seattle Fire Department

Yellow Umbrella Books

an imprint of Capstone Press
Mankato, Minnesota

A firefighter's day is busy.
There are so many things to do.

Firefighters check the truck.

They check the other tools, too.

Firefighters rush into action
when the alarm rings.

Sometimes firefighters
use tools to get to a fire.

They spray the fire with plenty of water.

Firefighters use helicopters
to fight forest fires.

They also dig around the fire to stop it from spreading.

Firefighters help when cars crash.

Firefighters also help people who are sick or hurt.

They carry the people to safety.

Firefighters help in other ways, too. They teach children about fighting fires.

They tell children what to do in case of a fire.

Firefighters also learn about new ways to fight fires. They practice what they have learned.

A firefighter's day is very busy. Thank you, firefighters, for all you do!

Words to Know/Index

alarm—a device with a bell, buzzer, or siren that warns people of danger; page 5

crash—an accident in which a vehicle hits something at a high speed; page 10

forest—a large area thickly covered with trees and plants; page 8

helicopter—an aircraft with large rotating blades on top that can take off and land in a small space; page 8

practice—to repeat an action regularly in order to learn or improve a skill; page 15

rush—to do something or go somewhere quickly; page 5

spray—to scatter liquid in very fine drops; page 7

truck—a large motor vehicle used for carrying items; fire trucks carry firefighters and their tools; page 3

Word Count: 136
Early-Intervention Level: 12